# Enid Blyton
# The toys go to the seaside

illustrated by Peter Lee

© ENID BLYTON 1973
ISBN 0 340 175206
Printed in England by
Sir Joseph Causton and Sons Ltd.,
London & Eastleigh.

Once upon a time the goblin Peeko put his head in at the nursery window and cried, 'Who wants a day at the seaside?'

The toys sat up with a jerk. They were all alone in the nursery, for Tom and Beryl, whose toys they were, had gone away to stay at their Granny's. The toys were really feeling rather dull. A day at the seaside sounded simply gorgeous!

'How do we go?' asked the pink rabbit.

'By bus,' said the goblin, grinning. 'My bus. I bought it yesterday. Penny each all the way there.'

'Oooh!' said sailor doll, longingly. 'I would like to see the sea. I've never been there — and it's dreadful to be a sailor doll and not to know what the sea is like, really it is!'

'Come on then,' said Peeko. 'Climb out of the window, all of you. There's plenty of room in the bus.'

So the pink rabbit, the sailor doll, the yellow duck, the walking-doll, the brown dog, and the blue teddy bear all climbed out of the window and got into the goblin's bus, which was standing on the path outside. The goblin took the wheel.

The bus gave a roar and a jolt that sent the pink rabbit nearly through the roof — and it was off! It was a fine journey to the sea. The goblin knew all the shortest cuts. It wasn't long before the sailor doll gave a yell and cried, 'The sea! The sea!'

'Pooh!' said the goblin 'That's just a duck-pond.'

'But aren't those gulls sailing on it?' asked the doll.

'No, *ducks*!' said Peeko.

'Quack, quack!' said the yellow toy duck, and laughed loudly at the sailor doll. After that the doll didn't say anything at all, not even when they came to the real sea and saw it glittering and shining in the sun. He was afraid it might be a duck-pond too — or an extra big puddle.

They all tumbled out of the bus and ran on to the beach. 'I'm off for a swim!' said the yellow duck.

'I'd like a sail in a boat!' said the sailor doll. 'Oh! There's a nice little boat over there, just my size.'

It belonged to a little boy. He had gone home to dinner and had forgotten to take his boat with him. The sailor doll ran to it, pushed it out to sea, jumped aboard and was soon off for a fine sail.

The pink rabbit thought he would like to
make a burrow for himself in the sand.
It was always so difficult to dig a burrow in
the nursery. So he began to dig, and
showered sand all over the blue teddy bear.

'Hey, hey, pink rabbit, what are you doing?' cried the bear. But the pink rabbit was already deep in the sandy tunnel, enjoying himself thoroughly, and didn't hear the bear's shout.

'I shall have a nap,' said the blue teddy bear. 'Don't disturb me, anybody.'

He lay down on the soft yellow sand and shut his eyes. Soon a deep growly snore was heard. The brown dog giggled and looked at the walking-doll. 'Shall we bury him in the sand?' he wuffed. 'He would be so surprised when he woke up and found himself a sandy bear.' 'Yes, let's,' said the doll. So they began to bury the sleeping teddy in the sand. They piled it over his legs, they piled it over his fat little tummy, they piled it over his arms. They didn't put any on his head, so all that could be seen of the bear was just his blunt blue snout sticking up. He really looked funny.

'I'm off for a walk,' said the walking-doll. 'This beach is a good place to stretch my legs. I never can walk very far in the nursery — only round and round and round.'

She set off over the beach, her long legs going back and forth. The brown dog was alone. What should he do?

'The sailor doll is sailing. The yellow duck
is swimming. The pink rabbit is burrowing.
The teddy bear is sleeping. The walking-doll
is walking. I think I will go and sniff
round for a big fat bone,' said the brown
dog. So off he went.

Now when Peeko the goblin came on to the beach two or three hours later, to tell the toys that it was time to go home, do you think he could see a single one? No! There didn't seem to be anyone in sight at all! Peeko was annoyed.

'Just like them to disappear when it's time to go home,' he said crossly. 'Well, I suppose I must wait for them, that's all. I'll sit down.'

Peeko looked for a nice place to sit down. He saw a soft-looking humpy bit of sand. It was really the teddy bear's tummy, buried in the sand, but he didn't know that. He walked over to the humpy bit and sat right down in the middle of it.

The blue bear woke up with a jump.

'Oooourrrrrrrr,' he growled, and sat up suddenly. The goblin fell over in a fright. The bear snapped at him and growled again. Then he saw it was Peeko. 'What do you mean by sitting down in the middle of me like that?' he said crossly.

'How should I know it was the middle of you when you were all buried in sand?' said Peeko.

'I wasn't,' said the bear, in surprise, for he had no idea he had been buried.

'You were,' said Peeko.

'I wasn't,' said the bear.

'Well, we can go on wasing and wasn'ting for ages,' said Peeko. 'Just tell me this, teddy — where in the world has everyone gone to? It's time to go home.'

'Is it really?' said the bear, astonished. 'Dear me, it seems as if we've only just come!'

'I don't see why you wanted to come at all if all you do is snore,' said Peeko. 'Waste of a penny I call it!'

'Well if you think that, I won't give you my penny,' said the bear at once.

'Don't be silly,' said the goblin.

'Look here bear, if we don't start soon it will be too late. What am I to do? I'd better go without you.'

'Oh no, don't do that,' said the bear in alarm. 'I'll soon get the others back. We have a special whistle that we use when it's time to go home.'

He pursed his teddy-bear mouth and whistled. It was a shrill, loud whistle, and every one of the toys heard it. You should have seen them rushing back to the beach!

The sailor doll sailed his ship proudly to the shore, jumped out, and pulled the ship on to the sand. He really did feel a sailor now!

The yellow duck came quacking and swimming in, bobbing up and down in delight. She waddled up the beach, and shook her feathers, sending a shower of drops all over Peeko, who was most annoyed. The walking-doll rushed back across the beach. The brown dog came running up, carrying an enormous bone in his mouth, very old and smelly. The toys looked at it in disgust.

'Where's the pink rabbit?' asked Peeko. 'He *would* be last!' The toys giggled.

Peeko was standing just at the entrance of the pink rabbit's burrow, but he didn't know he was! The toys knew what would happen — and it did!

The pink rabbit had heard the bear's whistle. He was coming back along his burrow. He suddenly shot out, all legs and sand — and Peeko felt his legs bumped hard, and he sat down very suddenly! The pink rabbit had come out in a great hurry, just between the goblin's legs. The toys laughed till they cried. Peeko was quite angry. 'First I sit on a hump that isn't a hump and get a dreadful fright!' he said. 'And then I get bowled over by a silly rabbit who comes out of the sand. Get into the bus, all of you, before I say I won't take you home.'

They all got into the bus. Most of them were tired and sleepy now, all except the teddy bear, who was very lively indeed — but then, he had been asleep all the time!

They climbed in at the nursery window.
They each gave Peeko a penny, and he
drove his bus away quietly, and parked it
under the lilac bush.

The toys crept into the cupboard and sat as still as could be.

And when Tom and Beryl came back the next day from their Granny's they *were* surprised to see how well and brown their toys all looked.

'Just as if they had been to the sea!' said Tom.

'Don't be silly Tom!' said Beryl.

But he wasn't silly, they had been to the sea!